mary-kateandashley

TWO of a kind ™

Bye-bye Boyfriend

Look for these

titles:

mary-kateandashley

TWO of a kind™

Bye-bye
Boyfriend

by Judy Katschke

from the series created by Robert Griffard
& Howard Adler

TED SMART

A PARACHUTE PRESS BOOK

A PARACHUTE PRESS BOOK
Parachute Publishing, L.L.C.
156 Fifth Avenue
Suite 325
NEW YORK
NY 10010

This edition produced for The Book People Ltd,
Hall Wood Avenue,
Haydock, St Helens, WA11 9UL
First published in the USA by HarperEntertainment 2000
First published in Great Britain by HarperCollins*Entertainment* 2003
HarperCollins*Entertainment* is an imprint of HarperCollins*Publishers* Ltd,
77-85 Fulham Palace Road, Hammersmith, London W6 8JB

The HarperCollins website address is
www.harpercollins.co.uk

ISBN 0 00 775043 9

Printed and bound in China

CHAPTER ONE

"Why do they call them morning announcements?" twelve-year-old Mary-Kate Burke whispered to her twin sister. "They should be 'yawning' announcements!"

"Shh," Ashley said, pointing to the front of the auditorium. "Here comes the Head!"

Mrs Pritchard, the headmistress of the White Oak Academy for Girls, smiled as she walked on to the stage. "Good morning, girls!" she announced.

"Good morning, Mrs Pritchard," Mary-Kate chanted with the other students.

The twins knew the drill at the White Oak Academy. It meant eating oatmeal each morning and sharing a bathroom with a dozen other girls. It also meant having the time of their lives!

"Hey, Mary-Kate?" Ashley whispered. "Who's the guy sitting on the stage? Behind Mrs Pritchard?"

Mary-Kate noticed the man with the grey hair and moustache, too. He wore a navy blue blazer and brown trousers. A maroon scarf was tied neatly round his neck.

"Probably the new physics teacher," Mary-Kate whispered back. "The last one just had a baby."

"We have a special announcement this morning," Mrs Pritchard said, looking over her glasses at her notes. "It is time once again for the annual White Oak Academy First Form school musical. As you know, each year White Oak teams up with the Harrington School for Boys to put on a show!"

A show? Mary-Kate's sleepy eyes flew wide open. Ever since she had played Tiger Lily in their Chicago school's production of *Peter Pan*, acting had become her passion. Besides softball and basketball, of course!

"This year the First Form musical will be *Bye Bye Birdie*," Mrs Pritchard said. "And no, girls, it's not about an endangered species . . ."

Mrs Pritchard paused so a few girls could laugh at her joke. Then she went on. "It's about a teenage girl who is picked to meet her favourite teen idol before he goes off to the army."

"What a cool show!" Ashley whispered to Mary-Kate. "Maybe I'll go for it, too."

Mary-Kate shot her sister a surprised glance. Ashley was great at ballet, cooking and maths. But when it came to singing, her sister could really clear a room!

"Ashley, this is a *musical*," Mary-Kate said. "You sing 'Happy Birthday' off-key!"

"But I *do* have acting experience!" Ashley said. "Remember the second grade play, *A Salute to the Solar System*? I played Saturn!"

"And you spun around so fast you threw up!" Mary-Kate reminded her.

"That was five years ago!" Ashley smiled as she tugged at her silver butterfly necklace. "Besides, if I get a great part, I might score some extra points with Ross!"

Mary-Kate grinned. It was no secret that sparks were flying between Ashley and Ross Lambert, a First Form student at the Harrington School for Boys. Ross wasn't exactly Ashley's boyfriend yet, but the butterfly necklace he gave her for their birthday was a pretty good sign!

"Now, girls," Mrs Pritchard said with a sigh. "I'll

admit that previous productions have not always gone smoothly. The snow machine in *The Sound of Music* caused a dreadful blizzard, and the costumes from *Cats* left hairballs – but this year will be different!"

Mary-Kate watched as Mrs Pritchard swept her arm in the direction of the mystery guest.

"I would like you all to meet this year's artist-in-residence," Mrs Pritchard said. "Mr Dale Boulderblatt!"

Mr Boulderblatt stood up and bowed.

"Boulderblatt." Campbell giggled to Mary-Kate. "Try saying that five times fast!"

"Mr Boulderblatt is a theatre director," Mrs Pritchard said. "He has directed several Broadway shows."

A real Broadway director at White Oak? Mary-Kate sat up straight. No way!

Dale Boulderblatt cleared his throat as he took over the microphone. "I would just like to say how pleased I am to be here at the Green Oak Academy for Girls!"

"Excuse me, that's White Oak," Mrs Pritchard corrected him politely. "The White Oak Academy for Girls."

"Yes, yes, of course," Mr Boulderblatt said quickly. "And may I just say that, although we're a long way from the Broadway lights – we're just a few short weeks away from a Dale Boulderblatt theatrical production!"

Mrs Pritchard encouraged the girls to applaud.

"I auditioned boys from the Harrington School yesterday," Mr Boulderblatt said. "And since we are dealing with a tight schedule, your auditions will be held tomorrow afternoon."

"Tomorrow?" Mary-Kate gasped.

"You may sing a song of your choice," Mr Boulderblatt went on. Then he rolled his eyes. "But please – no MTV!"

"Are there any questions for Mr Boulderblatt before we go to breakfast?" Mrs Pritchard asked the girls.

Mary-Kate's hand shot up. "What's the lead role in the play, Mr Boulderblatt?" she asked.

"That would be Kim McAfee," Mr Boulderblatt answered. "The starry-eyed teenager torn between her boyfriend, Hugo, and the hip-swivelling rock singer Conrad Birdie."

"And," Mrs Pritchard said, "the student who plays Kim will have her own dressing room!"

Excited whispers filled the auditorium.

"That's the part I'm going for!" Mary-Kate whispered to Campbell. "Kim!"

"I don't want to burst your bubble, Mary-Kate," Campbell said with a frown. "But you're going to have some stiff competition."

"What do you mean?" Mary-Kate asked.

"Two rows back is Valerie Metcalf," Campbell said. "Valerie played the lead in *Cats* last year. And she's done some cereal adverts where she lives in Los Angeles."

"Valerie is in my gym class," Mary-Kate said, surprised. "The teacher is always on her case for wearing platform sneakers. But I didn't know she could act."

Mary-Kate turned round and saw Valerie Metcalf coolly twisting her shiny black hair between her fingers. She was wearing a yellow cardigan with fake feathers and dark sunglasses – inside!

"I'm just warning you, Mary-Kate," Campbell said. "Valerie Metcalf is practically a star."

"Yeah," Mary-Kate joked. "But did she ever play Tiger Lily?"

Worried, Mary-Kate leaned back in her seat. She was used to competing in softball and basketball and even tetherball.

But on the stage?

That was a whole different ballgame!

CHAPTER TWO

This is going to be so cool, Ashley thought as she listened to Mr Boulderblatt and Mrs Pritchard talk about *Bye Bye Birdie.*

"The music you will need for your auditions will probably be available at the music library," Mrs Pritchard went on. "Mrs Wilcox, the librarian, will help you find it."

Oh, boy, Ashley thought. *If auditions are tomorrow, I'd better get busy!*

Not that she wasn't busy already. Ashley was a reporter for the school paper, the White Oak *Acorn.* Her roommate Phoebe Cahill was First Form editor.

"Thank you for your attention, girls," Mrs Pritchard said. She looked down at her notes. "The oatmeal flavour of the day will be . . . cherry vanilla."

Everyone jumped up from her seat. Announcing the oatmeal flavour was Mrs Pritchard's way of saying the meeting was dismissed!

"Wait up, Mary-Kate," Ashley called as she followed her sister up the aisle. "I have the most awesome idea!"

"What?" Mary-Kate asked.

"Let's audition *together*!" Ashley said, her eyes shining. "We can do that number those twins sang in *The Parent Trap*. 'Let's get together – yeah, yeah, yeah—'"

"Ashley, we want to get parts in the play," Mary-Kate groaned. "Not get run out of town!"

"Just a suggestion," Ashley shrugged. She spun round when someone tapped her shoulder.

It was Phoebe, dressed in her usual vintage clothes. Today she wore a stretchy cardigan, cropped pants and saddle shoes. Her curly dark hair was tied back in a blue scarf that matched the frames of her cat-eye glasses.

"Hey, Phoebe," Ashley said. "What's up?"

Phoebe held up her reporter pad. "We must interview Dale Boulderblatt for the White Oak *Acorn*," she said excitedly. "He's practically famous!"

"The paper?" Ashley gulped. She was so psyched about being an actress that she forgot about being a reporter!

Ashley gave Mary-Kate a little wave and followed Phoebe. Mr Boulderblatt was standing alone in front of the stage and writing in a schedule book.

"Mr Boulderblatt?" Phoebe said. "My name is Phoebe Cahill and this is Ashley Burke. We're reporters—"

Mr Boulderblatt held out his hand like a lollipop man. "Stop!" He yanked off his glasses and wiped them on his tie. He put them back on and stared at Phoebe. "I knew it! I just knew it!"

"Knew what?" Phoebe asked, confused.

"Young lady, is that a vintage, nineteen-sixty, one hundred per cent Ban-Lon cardigan you are wearing?" Mr Boulderblatt asked.

Phoebe looked down at her white sweater. "Actually it's nineteen fifty-nine," she said. "But my pedal pushers are from nineteen sixty. And my saddle shoes are from – I think the same year Elvis Presley was on the *Ed Sullivan Show*."

"You know Ed Sullivan?" Mr Boulderblatt gasped.

Ashley wrinkled her nose. "Who's Ed Sullivan?"

"Ed Sullivan used to have a popular TV show,"

Mr Boulderblatt explained. "His guests could be anyone from a Metropolitan Opera star to a dancing bear in a tutu!"

Ashley tried to look impressed.

"In fact, Mr Sullivan's character is a big part in *Bye Bye Birdie*," Mr Boulderblatt said. "But enough about him – where *did* you get those fabulous fashion relics?"

"Oh, all sorts of vintage shops," Phoebe said. "The Musty Closet, Grandma's Attic. I've even made a few of my own outfits – using vintage fabrics, of course."

A grin spread across Mr Boulderblatt's face. "I've found her!" He swooned. "My student wardrobe supervisor!"

"Me?" Phoebe asked.

"Her?" Ashley gasped.

"Oh, yes!" Mr Boulderblatt told Phoebe. "*Bye Bye Birdie* takes place in the early sixties. And you're already an expert on the styles of that time."

"What will I have to do?" Phoebe asked.

"You'll work closely with Mrs Tuttle, the sewing teacher, who will act as our seamstress," he said. "But whatever you do, don't mention those cat costumes from the year before. She feels directly responsible for those nasty hairballs!"

Ashley watched her roommate think it over.

No way will Phoebe take a job in the school play, Ashley thought. *The* Acorn *always comes first.*

"Okay, I'll do it!" Phoebe blurted.

"Huh?" Ashley gasped.

"Fabulous!" Mr Boulderblatt said. "Meet me in the Performing Arts Centre during the midday break. I'll tell you the type of costumes I have in mind for the show."

Phoebe was jumping with excitement as they ran out of the auditorium. "Ashley, do you believe it?" she asked. "I'm going to be a costume designer!"

"But what about the school paper?" Ashley asked. "You're up to your elbows in reviews and articles!"

"It's good to be well rounded," Phoebe said. "Besides, it would be a great experience for *you* to write most of the articles for the next few weeks!"

Ashley stopped walking. "Phoebe, I can't do that," she said. "I'm auditioning for *Bye Bye Birdie,* too."

"You?" Phoebe stopped walking, too. "But you sing 'Happy Birthday' off-key!"

Ashley rolled her eyes. What did "Happy Birthday" have to do with *Bye Bye Birdie* anyway?

"I'm sure there's a part for me," Ashley said. She

11

put her arm round Phoebe's shoulders. "Especially now that I'm friends with the student costume supervisor."

Ashley and Phoebe walked to the main building for breakfast. But as they neared the dining hall, Ashley saw a crowd of girls standing in front of a notice board. Mary-Kate was there, too.

"What's going on?" Ashley asked her sister.

"It's the Harrington cast list," Mary-Kate answered. "Check out all the boys who are in the play!"

"Boys?" Ashley stood on her toes to get a closer look. She recognized a few names.

"Our cousin Jeremy is playing Ed Sullivan!" Ashley said.

"Who's Ed Sullivan?" Mary-Kate asked.

"I'll explain later," Ashley said.

"Oh, neat!" Phoebe cried. "Perry will be playing the piano in the play."

Ashley gave Phoebe a high five. She knew her roommate liked Perry Joplin. He played musical instruments and wrote poetry. He even liked vintage clothes—just like Phoebe!

Ashley tilted her head as she eyeballed the list. Then she saw something that made her jaw drop. "Wow!" she gasped. "Ross is playing Conrad Birdie, the teen idol. I didn't know he was so talented!"

"He doesn't have to be talented," a cool voice said.

Ashley spun round. A dark-haired girl in a feathered yellow sweater was standing with her arms folded across her chest. Her pink, glossed lips were curved in a smile.

"He just has to be a *hunk*," the girl said. "Just like Kim has to be . . . *pretty*!"

Ashley watched as the girl strutted into the dining room. "Who was that?" she asked.

"Valerie Metcalf," Mary-Kate said. "Last year she played the lead hairball in *Cats*. This year she'll probably play Kim."

"Or Big Bird!" Phoebe joked.

Ashley didn't laugh. Valerie was pretty and confident. Maybe pretty and confident enough to flirt with Ross!

"You mean to tell me Ross will be spending half his time with girls like Valerie Metcalf?" Ashley said.

"Yeah, so?" Mary-Kate asked.

"So?" Ashley cried. "So I have to get a part in *Bye Bye Birdie*. If it's the last thing I do!"

CHAPTER THREE

"Circle skirts, mohair sweaters and cha-cha heels!" Phoebe said. She held up her fashion sketches one by one. "This show will be a blast from the past!"

"Like your wardrobe!" Ashley joked.

It was the night before the auditions. Phoebe had invited Mary-Kate, Campbell and Wendy to her and Ashley's room to munch on pretzels and cheese dip and listen to Phoebe's original soundtrack of *Bye Bye Birdie*.

"I saw the movie on TV," Phoebe said. "Conrad Birdie gives Kim a symbolic kiss on the *Ed Sullivan Show*. It's his way of saying goodbye to all his fans."

"Kiss?" Ashley practically stood up. "You mean Ross will have to kiss a girl? Like Valerie Metcalf?"

14

Phoebe shook her head. "When Conrad tries to kiss Kim, her boyfriend, Hugo, runs onstage and socks him in the nose!"

"Are you still going to audition for the role of Kim, Mary-Kate?" Wendy asked.

"You bet!" Mary-Kate said. "Valerie Metcalf isn't going to stop me from reaching my goal."

Phoebe held up a vinyl record by its edges. "Okay, everyone – here it is," she announced. "*Bye Bye Birdie!*"

The girls sat in a circle round Phoebe's portable vintage record player. Phoebe carefully laid the record on the turntable and flicked a switch. A needle attached to an arm lowered itself onto the record as it began to spin.

"Right after the overture is Kim's first song," Phoebe explained. "It's called, 'How Lovely to Be a Woman'."

Mary-Kate wiggled closer to the record player. She leaned forward and listened as Kim began to sing.

Mary-Kate blinked hard. The song was all about growing up. But Kim didn't want to grow up because she would be smarter or stronger or more mature. All she wanted to do was wear make-up and have boys whistle at her! Was she serious?

"Stop the music!" Mary-Kate ordered. She

15

grabbed the arm of the record player. "Stop the music!"

"What's wrong?" Ashley asked.

"Did you hear that?" Mary-Kate asked, pointing to the record player. "To Kim, being a woman means wearing mascara and high heels and chasing boys!"

Ashley shrugged. "Sounds okay to me!"

"Well, not to me!" Mary-Kate declared. "If I sang a song like that, I'd be the joke of my softball team."

"I'd rethink this if I were you, Mary-Kate," Ashley said. "What about your passion for acting?"

"What about my *reputation*?" Mary-Kate groaned.

"There must be another part you can play," Phoebe said. Her eyes lit up. "I know – why don't you try out for Rosie? Rosie is the dynamic secretary. She's scheming and headstrong, and nowhere does she sing about high heels!"

"Scheming, huh?" Mary-Kate said. "That's better than boy crazy."

"Then go for it, Mary-Kate," Campbell said.

Mary-Kate gave it a thought. Okay, Rosie wouldn't be the starring role – but it would be a part she could be proud of. And that was important, too!

"I'm going for Rosie," Mary-Kate declared. "Valerie is probably going to land the part of Kim anyway."

"Bite your tongue!" Ashley cried. Then she smiled around the room. "Okay, you guys. What about me? Who should I audition for?"

Mary-Kate cringed as her sister jumped up and began to sing: "Getting to know you! Getting to know all about you!"

"Ashley!" Phoebe interrupted.

"What?" Ashley stopped singing and blinked.

"There is a part for you," Phoebe said. "You could play Conrad's adoring fan."

"Conrad's adoring fan – I like that!" Ashley said excitedly. "What's her name?"

"Um – she doesn't really have a name," Phoebe explained. "She's one of the girls in a crowd."

"A crowd scene?" Ashley cried. "No way!"

"What's wrong with a crowd scene?" Mary-Kate asked, reaching for another pretzel.

"Because Ross Lambert has the lead. And if Ross can have a major part, so can I!" Ashley said firmly. "I'm going for the part of Kim!"

CHAPTER FOUR

"Take any available seats," Mr Boulderblatt told the girls as they filed into the theatre the next afternoon. "We're going to start in a few minutes."

Ashley's circle skirt swished as she made her way to the seats. She was so excited about auditioning for the part of Kim that she had borrowed an authentic fifties outfit from Phoebe.

"Hey, Ashley," Mary-Kate called from the second row. "Over here!"

With her sheet music under her arm, Ashley sat down next to Mary-Kate.

"What was that crunch?" Mary-Kate asked.

"Oh, that's my petticoat!" Ashley explained.

"What's it made of – corn chips?" Mary-Kate joked.

"Very funny," Ashley said.

Campbell and Wendy walked in wearing softball uniforms and catcher's gloves.

"Don't tell me I'm missing softball practice," Mary-Kate said as the two took seats in her row.

"Not!" Campbell said. "Wendy and I are singing 'You've Gotta Have Heart'. It's from the musical *Damn Yankees*."

Mary-Kate looked at Wendy's uniform. "Since when do you play softball, Wendy?" she asked.

"Since I borrowed your uniform!" Wendy turned around to reveal Mary-Kate's number. "Thanks, Mary-Kate!"

More girls came into the theatre. Ashley spotted their friends Elise Van Hook, Cheryl Miller and Summer Sorenson. But there was one girl she didn't see anywhere . . .

"Where's Valerie Metcalf?" Ashley asked.

"You mean Miss Hollywood?" Campbell rolled her eyes. "She probably wants to make a grand entrance!"

Ashley gripped her sheet music. She didn't care how many cereal adverts Valerie Metcalf did. She was going to get the part of Kim if she had to stand on her head and spit pennies!

"Okay, girls," Mr Boulderblatt called out. "I want

to thank you all for your punctuality. May I just say that being on time is a crucial part of working in the theatre?"

Hear that, Valerie? Ashley thought with a smirk.

Mr Boulderblatt paced back and forth with a clipboard under his arm. "I am sure that with the right amount of hard work and talent, we can surely put on a memorable and entertaining show!" he said.

Ashley glanced down at the sheet music on Mary-Kate's lap. It was "Put on a Happy Face" from *Bye Bye Birdie.*

"Do you think Dad will come to the show?" Ashley whispered to Mary-Kate.

"Probably not." Mary-Kate sighed. "Chicago isn't exactly a hop, skip and a jump away from New Hampshire."

Missing their college professor dad was the worst part of boarding school. But Kevin Burke's voice was always inside their heads – usually telling them to do their homework or brush their teeth!

"Let's begin!" Mr Boulderblatt interrupted Ashley's thoughts with a booming voice. The director took a seat in the first row and signalled to Perry Joplin.

Perry was wearing cuffed blue jeans, red

moccasins and a black-and-white Beethoven T-shirt. He took his place at the piano and cracked his knuckles.

"First up will be . . ." Mr Boulderblatt checked his clipboard. "Cecilia Marie Lakehurst!"

"That's me!" A girl with red hair and freckles jumped up from the third row. She wore a tuxedo-style leotard and a top hat. In her hand was a sparkly silver-and-black cane.

As Cecilia handed her music to Perry, Ashley sighed with relief. She didn't want to be the first to audition. Or the last. Somewhere in the middle would be okay.

Cecilia's shoes made tap-tap-tapping noises as she walked to the middle of the stage.

"I'd like to audition for the part of Kim," Cecilia announced.

Ashley leaned over to Mary-Kate. "Do you think it's too late for *me* to tap-dance?" she whispered.

"Don't even think about it!" Mary-Kate warned.

Perry's shoulders moved up and down as he played Cecilia's song, "Puttin' On the Ritz". Cecilia tapped and sang her heart out.

The theatre echoed with Cecilia's taps. But when Cecilia kicked out her right leg, her tap shoe went flying into the audience!

"Owww – my nose!" a girl in the back cried out.

"S-s-sorry!" Cecilia stammered. She hobbled off the stage while Mr Boulderblatt wrote on his clipboard.

Wow, Ashley thought. *Anything can happen up there!*

"Next to audition will be Campbell Smith and Wendy Linden," Mr Boulderblatt called out.

"Go for it!" Ashley cheered as her two friends ran on to the stage. Campbell and Wendy swayed back and forth in their softball uniforms while Perry played the introduction. Then they began to belt out their song.

"Hey, they're not bad!" Ashley told Mary-Kate.

"And I thought the only baseball song was 'Take Me Out to the Ball Game'!" Mary-Kate said.

Campbell and Wendy got down on their knees for the big finish: "You've gotta have heaaaart!"

Campbell spread out her arms and accidentally whacked Wendy in the mouth with her catcher's glove. Wendy stumbled back and forth a bit but she seemed to be okay.

"Thank you, Campbell and Wendy," Mr Boulderblatt muttered as he scribbled on his clipboard.

Ashley made room for Wendy and Campbell as they returned to their seats.

"I guess I got carried away," Campbell mumbled.

"Next will be . . ." Mr Boulderblatt started to say.

Ashley turned to Wendy and Campbell. "You guys were great," she whispered. "I really liked that—"

"Ashley Burke!" Mr Boulderblatt finished.

"Huh?" Ashley's head snapped around.

"That's you, Ashley!" Mary-Kate whispered. "You're on!"

Ashley thought she'd be nervous when Mr Boulderblatt called her. But instead she was totally psyched.

This is it, Ashley thought excitedly. *I'm going to go up there, sing my lungs out, and ace the role of Kim!*

Ashley's petticoat rustled and her ponytail bounced as she made her way to the stage. She could see Perry smiling at her from the piano.

After handing Perry her music sheet, Ashley stood in the centre of the stage.

"What are you going to sing, Ashley Burke?" Mr Boulderblatt asked, not looking up from his clipboard.

"'One Boy'," Ashley answered. "The song that Kim sings to her boyfriend, Hugo."

While Perry set up the music, Ashley looked around the theatre. She could see Mary-Kate and her friends giving her thumbs-up signs. But then Ashley saw someone else. Sitting in the back of the theatre with his legs stretched out in the aisle was Ross!

Ross waved at Ashley and her heart began to pound.

How can I sing about wanting a boy – when the boy who I want is sitting right there? she thought.

The music began to play. Ashley opened her mouth to sing.

But nothing came out!

CHAPTER FIVE

"Ashley?" Mr Boulderblatt called out. "Aren't you going to sing 'One Boy'?"

Ashley gulped as she thought of Ross in the back of the theatre.

"Uh-oh," Mary-Kate told Campbell and Wendy. "Ashley is choking!"

"We're waiting, Ashley," Mr Boulderblatt said.

Mary-Kate bit her lip. She could practically see the vein in Ashley's neck throbbing.

Perry struck a chord and Ashley opened her mouth. Then . . .

"CROOAK!"

The theatre was silent. A few girls broke out into sniggers.

"Thank you, Ashley," Mr Boulderblatt said. "But we must move on. Next!"

Ashley's face turned tomato red. She spun round on her saddle shoe heel and hurried off the stage.

"What happened up there?" Mary-Kate demanded after Ashley sank into her seat. "Just a few minutes ago you couldn't wait to audition!"

"That's before I saw Ross in the audience," Ashley muttered. She sank lower in her seat. "Now I'll never get the part of Kim!"

Mary-Kate wondered if Ashley would get *any* part now! "Forget it, Ashley," she said. "Neither of us will get the part of Kim. It's going to go to Valerie, so deal with it!"

As if on cue, the door to the theatre swung open. Valerie Metcalf posed at the door, then strutted in wearing a tiny black dress and rhinestone-studded sunglasses.

"Hello, everyone!" Valerie called out. She propped her shades on top of her head. "I'm ready for my audition!"

Valerie handed Mr Boulderblatt an 8 x 10 glossy photograph and a resumé. "My agent's name is on the back," she added.

Mr Boulderblatt tossed the picture and resumé

26

aside. "I was just about to call your name, Valerie," he said. "Why don't you give Perry your music and we'll begin."

Mary-Kate watched as Miss Hollywood tossed Perry her sheet music. But instead of running up on stage, Valerie began rolling her head and making noises like a walrus!

"MWA-AAAAH! MWA-AAAAAH!"

"What is she auditioning for?" Campbell asked. *"National Geographic?"*

"Miss Metcalf, what on earth are you doing?" Mr Boulderblatt asked.

"Warm-up exercises!" Valerie said, still rolling her head. "An actor must prepare, you know."

"Well, prepare to leave this theatre if you don't start right away!" Mr Boulderblatt warned.

Valerie's head snapped back up. "I'm ready!"

"What part are you auditioning for?" Mr Boulderblatt asked, looking down at his clipboard.

"Are you serious?" Valerie chuckled as she walked on to the stage. "I'm auditioning for the lead! Kim McAfee."

"Oh, great," Ashley groaned.

Valerie motioned for Perry to begin.

Mary-Kate and the others watched as Valerie began waving her arms in the air. "I had a dreeeeeeam!" she began to sing. "A dream about you, ba-by!"

"As much as I hate to admit it, she's good," Mary-Kate said as Valerie burst into "Everything's Coming up Roses".

"You're right," Ashley sighed. "Valerie is going to get the part of Kim McAfee. And I have to deal with it."

Although no one applauded when Valerie finished, she took a dramatic, sweeping bow. Then she turned and gestured to Perry. Surprised, Perry nodded to the audience.

"What a ham!" Campbell mumbled.

Looking pleased with herself, Valerie took a seat in the row behind Mary-Kate and Ashley.

Mr Boulderblatt turned back to his notes. "And next we will hear from . . . "

Wow, Mary-Kate thought. *I feel sorry for the person who has to follow that act.*

"Mary-Kate Burke!"

Mary-Kate felt sick. Why her?

"Go for it, Mary-Kate," Ashley whispered. "You're auditioning for Rosie – not for Kim!"

Ashley had a point. Mary-Kate took a deep breath and stood up. Then she walked up to the stage and handed Perry her music.

"I suppose you're auditioning for Kim, too," Mr Boulderblatt said with a little sigh.

"No, Mr Boulderblatt," Mary-Kate said. "I'm auditioning for Rosie. Hit it, Perry!"

The audience seemed like a big blur as Mary-Kate stared into it. She could feel her heart pounding against her rib cage. But when the music began to play, Mary-Kate forgot the butterflies in her stomach and began to sing. She smiled and strutted back and forth across the stage. She even sat on top of the piano and pretended to sing to Perry!

When the song was over, the audience went wild. Mary-Kate could see Ashley standing up and cheering. Even Mr Boulderblatt was smiling as he scribbled on his clipboard.

They like me! Mary-Kate thought as she took a bow. *They really, really like me!*

"Thank you, Mary-Kate!" Mr Boulderblatt said, still smiling. "For that energetic little number."

Mary-Kate smiled. She grabbed her music and hurried back to her seat.

"You were a hit, Mary-Kate," Ashley squealed.

"Way to go!" Campbell said.

"Thanks," Mary-Kate said. But from the corner of her eye she could see Valerie Metcalf glaring at her.

What's her problem? Mary-Kate wondered. *After*

all, it's not like we're going for the same part.

The twins sat through the rest of the acts. After Cheryl Miller sang "There's No Business Like Show Business", the auditions were over.

"Thank you, everyone," Mr Boulderblatt announced from the stage. "Since we are so pressed for time, the cast list will go up outside the theatre promptly at five o'clock."

Mary-Kate looked at her watch. Five o'clock was just one hour away. "Where should we wait for the verdict?" she asked Ashley and her friends.

"Anywhere near a vending machine," Wendy said. "When I'm this nervous, only dark chocolate with almonds will do!"

Many of the girls hung around in the common room to kill time. While Valerie sat in a comfy chair reading the *Hollywood Reporter*, the twins and their friends flipped through old copies of *Seventeen* and *Calling All Girls*. Phoebe had taken the 1950s issues out of the school library for costume research.

"I can't believe they wore penny loafers in the nineteen fifties!" Ashley said, pointing to an old pimple cream ad. "They wear penny loafers today."

"Except now they're up to a dime!" Mary-Kate joked.

Phoebe jabbed her finger on a photograph of a

model wearing a pink chiffon dress. "I'm going to choose soft, feminine styles for Kim," she said. "Lots of chiffon and mohair and—"

"Just keep in mind, Phoebe," Valerie interrupted from her chair. "I look best in cool tones!"

The girls spun around. Valerie was grinning at them over her copy of the *Hollywood Reporter*.

"She's so sure she's playing Kim," Ashley mumbled.

"Well, if she *does* play Kim," Phoebe whispered slyly, "I'll make sure to put extra starch in her petticoats!"

As the girls giggled, Mary-Kate glanced at the clock on the wall. It was three minutes to five o'clock.

"The list is going up!" Mary-Kate squealed.

Valerie joined the stampede to the Performing Arts Centre. Sure enough, the casting list was hanging up on a notice board outside the theatre.

"Yay! Yippee!" Elise Van Hook was jumping up and down excitedly. "I'm playing Ursula! I'm playing Ursula!"

Elise stopped jumping and wrinkled her nose. "Who's Ursula?"

"Congratulations, Elise!" Mary-Kate said as she and Ashley wiggled through the crowd towards the notice board.

Ashley ran her finger down the list. "Campbell,

Wendy, Summer and Kristen are playing the telephone girls!"

Mary-Kate heard Campbell and Wendy shriek. She smiled nervously as she looked for her own name on the list.

"Tatiana Riccio is playing Mrs McAfee," Mary-Kate read. "And Cheryl Miller is playing—"

"Who?" Ashley said, craning her neck.

"Rosie," Mary-Kate said quietly. Her heart sank. Cheryl got the role she auditioned for. Which probably meant that there was no role for her!

I'm not even in the play, Mary-Kate thought sadly. But just as she was turning to leave, Ashley let out a huge shriek—

"Mary-Kate! Mary-Kate! You've got the part of *Kim*!"

CHAPTER SIX

"K-K-Kim?" Mary-Kate stammered. "Did you say K-Kim?"

Ashley stared at her sister. She wasn't moving or blinking! "Omigosh!" she said. "Mary-Kate is in shock!"

Ashley began shaking Mary-Kate's arm. "Mary-Kate, I can't believe it—you got the lead! You got the lead!"

"And your own dressing room!" Wendy added.

"But I didn't go for the lead!" Mary-Kate protested.

The door to the theatre swung open and Mr Boulderblatt walked out.

"There must be some mistake," Mary-Kate told Ashley. "I'm going to talk to Mr Boulderblatt."

Ashley shook her head as she followed Mary-Kate. Why wasn't her sister happier?

"Excuse me, Mr Boulderblatt," Mary-Kate said. "But I never tried out for the part of Kim."

"I know that," Mr Boulderblatt said. "But I thought you'd be perfect for the role."

"But Kim and I are nothing alike!" Mary-Kate argued.

"Alike?" Mr Boulderblatt chuckled. "Are you saying you wouldn't play Peter Pan unless you could fly? Or the Cheshire Cat unless you had whiskers? Hmmm?"

"Now that you mention it . . ." Mary-Kate said slowly.

"I know you'll do a fine job," Mr Boulderblatt said with a smile. "And I know a natural when I see one."

"A natural?" Valerie cried as she marched over to Mr Boulderblatt. "What am I – chicken liver?"

"Your audition was very good, too," Mr Boulderblatt said. "That's why I made you Kim's understudy."

Valerie held her chest and swayed dramatically. "You mean I have to hope that Mary-Kate gets ill or breaks her arm so that I can play Kim?" she wailed.

"Take it or leave it," Mr Boulderblatt sighed.

"I'll take it," Valerie groaned. She turned to the other girls. "But I'll have everyone here know that I did a Cornflakes advert last summer!"

"She got milk all over her chin," Campbell muttered.

Ashley ran back to the casting list. She still hadn't found out who *she* was playing. But after checking the list once, twice, even three times, Ashley began to panic. Her name was nowhere to be found!

"Mr Boulderblatt?" Ashley called as she ran over to the director. "Someone must have accidentally left my name off the list. What part will I be playing?"

"No part, I'm afraid, Ashley," Mr Boulderblatt said. "Maybe next year. When you get over that . . . cold."

"But I don't have a cold!" Ashley insisted. "Can't I even play one of Conrad's fans?"

Mr Boulderblatt shook his head. "Even the fans have to sing," he said. "And singing doesn't seem to be your . . . strong point."

Ashley felt like the world had just come to an end. She had gone from trying out for the lead to getting nothing.

Zero. Zip. Zilch.

Oh, well, Ashley thought. *At least Mary-Kate will be playing Kim. And not Valerie Metcalf!*

"Congratulations, Mary-Kate," Ashley said with a smile. "I'm so proud of you . . . and relieved!"

"Relieved?" Mary-Kate asked.

"Sure!" Ashley began to whisper. "At least now I won't have to worry about Ross falling for Valerie!"

"Well, don't chill out too fast," Mary-Kate said. "Because if I get hurt or ill, Valerie takes my place."

Ashley's eyes popped wide open.

ill, Mary-Kate!" she cried. "You've got to take vitamin C every morning. And use antibacterial hand gel after you touch a doorknob. And don't forget to wear knee pads when you Rollerblade on campus."

Mary-Kate was laughing, but Ashley was dead serious. Valerie Metcalf could not get the role of Kim McAfee!

"Now listen carefully, girls," Mr Boulderblatt announced. "The first rehearsal schedules will be posted before breakfast tomorrow morning. If you miss a rehearsal without a solid excuse or a pass from a teacher or the school doctor—you're out of the show!"

"And I thought our softball coach was tough!" Campbell muttered. "Little did I know."

Ashley was about to congratulate some other girls when she saw Ross. He was walking towards them with a smile.

"Ross, what are you doing here?" Ashley asked, pleasantly surprised. "I thought you went back to Harrington after the rehearsals."

"And miss the posting of the White Oak list?" Ross smiled. "No way!"

"Then you probably saw I'm not in the play." Ashley sighed. "I suppose there are no parts for frogs. Croak."

"Cheer up," Ross said with a grin. "You're the cutest frog I ever saw."

Ashley's heart soared.

I think Ross still likes me! she thought. *How stupid of me to worry about other girls.*

Mary-Kate walked over to Ashley and Ross. She still looked pretty surprised about getting the lead.

"Congratulations, Mary-Kate," Ross said. "I think you'll make an awesome Kim."

"Thanks, Ross!" Mary-Kate said. "And congratulations to you for getting the part of Conrad."

"Hey, it was nothing," Ross said. He turned to Ashley. "The last van to Harrington leaves in an hour. How about a game of Frisbee on the lawn?"

"Sure!" Ashley said. "Want to join us, Mary-Kate?"

"Can't!" Mary-Kate said. "I want to check out this script and see what I'm in for."

"Come to think of it," Ross said slowly. "I'd better check out that script myself."

"Let's do it!" Mary-Kate said with a shrug.

"But what about our Frisbee game?" Ashley asked Ross.

"Some other time, okay?" Ross said. He began walking away with Mary-Kate. "See you, Ashley!"

Ashley's mouth dropped open as Ross and Mary-Kate went off together. Without her!

"Hmmm," Ashley mumbled under her breath. "Maybe I shouldn't get too relaxed!"

CHAPTER SEVEN

"Thanks for helping me with my lines, Ross," Mary-Kate said. "We're already halfway through the script."

Four days had passed since Mary-Kate had landed the role of Kim in *Bye Bye Birdie*. Just a few minutes before rehearsal, Mary-Kate and Ross were sitting on a bench in the campus square with their scripts on their laps.

"I can't wait until we run through our big scene at the end," Ross said. He highlighted one of his lines with a yellow marker. "You know, where Kim and Conrad come together on the *Ed Sullivan Show*."

"Let's check it out!" Mary-Kate said, flipping to the end. Ross looked over her shoulder as she began to read out loud: "The directions say that Kim comes out from backstage and recites her speech."

Mary-Kate read Kim's speech to herself. It wasn't very long.

"Then what?" Ross asked.

Mary-Kate continued to read. "Then Conrad leans over and plants a . . . plants a . . ."

With both hands Mary-Kate raised the script to her face. Did she see what she thought she saw?

"What?" Ross asked.

"A kiss," Mary-Kate finished. She looked at Ross. "Conrad plants a kiss on Kim's . . . lips."

"You mean . . . for real?" Ross gasped. He seemed lost in thought. "Wow. Ashley's going to flip."

Ashley was just one of Mary-Kate's worries. She had kissed a boy before – but not in front of hundreds of people!

"This doesn't seem right," Mary-Kate said. "Phoebe said Hugo jumps on stage and breaks the whole thing up!"

Ross grabbed the script and began to read. "He does! It says Hugo enters stage left. He sneaks up behind Conrad, taps him on the shoulder, and lands a punch on his nose!"

"Good!" Mary-Kate sighed.

"Sure," Ross joked. "It's not your nose!"

Mary-Kate giggled. "Whoever typed the directions must have made a mistake," she said. "When the rehearsal begins we'll just ask Mr Boulderblatt."

Ross shrugged. "Whatever!"

Mary-Kate could tell that Ross was trying to act supercool about the kiss. But she was pretty sure that he was relieved, too. He wanted to kiss Ashley, not her.

And that's fine with me, Mary-Kate thought. She looked at her watch and gasped.

"Hey, we'd better head to the rehearsals," Mary-Kate said, "Or it'll be Bye-Bye Mary-Kate and Ross!"

"And that about wraps it up for today," Mr Boulderblatt called out after the rehearsal that afternoon. "I must say, everything seems to be going well. Any questions?"

Mary-Kate raised her hand slowly.

"Um, I noticed that in the final scene, Kim and Conrad kiss," she said. "They don't *really* kiss, do they?"

"Oh, sure they do," Mr Boulderblatt said. "Until Hugo breaks it up, of course."

"But . . . in the movie Hugo stops it from happening," Mary-Kate said.

"My dear, this is not the Hollywood movie," Mr Boulderblatt said. "This is a Dale Boulderblatt theatrical production, and I say Conrad Birdie kisses Kim."

Valerie's hand shot up. "If Mary-Kate has a problem with the scene, I'll do it," she declared. "And all the other scenes, too!"

"I don't have a problem with it!" Mary-Kate snapped.

"Me neither," Ross said quickly.

"You can save the kiss for the dress rehearsal next week," Mr Boulderblatt told Mary-Kate and Ross. "You don't have to practise it yet."

"Unless they *want* to!" Jeremy called out.

Everyone sniggered.

"That's so funny I forgot to laugh," Mary-Kate muttered. How could she kiss a boy in front of the entire school and a lot of strangers, too?

And what is Ashley going to think when I kiss the boy of her dreams? Mary-Kate wondered. She looked around for the boy who was playing Hugo. Raymond Ferrer was sitting in the row behind her.

"Hey, Raymond," Mary-Kate whispered, leaning back. "When you run onstage to break up the kiss, remember – we want speed – not accuracy!"

CHAPTER EIGHT

"We love you Conrad! Oh, yes we dooooooo!"

Ashley pressed her ear against the theatre door. She sighed as she heard the chorus rehearsing their number.

"They don't love Conrad," Ashley mumbled to herself. "I do!"

The singing stopped. Ashley checked the clock and stepped away from the door. Every afternoon for the past five days Ashley had waited for her friends and sister outside the theatre door.

"Five... four... three... two... one..." Ashley counted down under her breath.

The door flew open and the cast poured out. Ashley could see Mary-Kate and Ross walking

43

together and checking out their notes.

"Thanks for helping me with that song, Ross," Mary-Kate was saying. "Let's go over your song tomorrow."

"It's a date!" Ross said.

Date? Ashley gulped as she tugged at her silver butterfly necklace.

"Hi, Ross!" Ashley called out.

Ross gave Ashley a little wave. "Hi, Ashley!" he said. "Got to run!"

That did it!

Ashley grabbed Mary-Kate by the elbow.

"Hey, watch it!" Mary-Kate complained. "That's my pitching arm!"

"Why should you care about softball?" Ashley asked. "You've obviously found a new love!"

"You mean acting?" Mary-Kate asked.

"I mean – Ross!" Ashley snapped. "Why have you been spending so much time with him lately?"

Mary-Kate snatched her arm back. "Ross and I just work well together, that's all."

"Oh, yeah?" Ashley sneered. "And what do you do when you're not working? Bowling? The movies? Miniature golf?"

"I hate miniature golf, and you know it," Mary-Kate snapped. "And what's up with you, anyway? I thought you were happy that I got the part of Kim!"

"I was," Ashley admitted. "I just didn't want you to enjoy it *that* much."

Mary-Kate heaved a big sigh. "Look, Ashley, I am enjoying it," she said. "In fact, I'm having the time of my life!"

Ashley gave Mary-Kate a pained look. Did she have to rub it in?

"And it's not because of Ross," Mary-Kate said firmly. "I just love acting, that's all. I love singing and pretending to be someone else . . . besides you, of course."

"Oh," Ashley said in a tiny voice. She had a feeling Mary-Kate was being sincere.

"Besides," Mary-Kate said. "Don't you even trust your own sister?"

Ashley felt like she had shrunk two feet. How could she not trust Mary-Kate? They'd been there for each other since day one. Even before!

"Look, I'm sorry," Ashley said. "I should have known you wouldn't try to steal Ross away from me."

"I steal bases, not boyfriends!" Mary-Kate joked.

The twins smiled as they walked out of the theatre.

"And remember," Mary-Kate added. "Hugo is

my boyfriend in the play, not Conrad."

"That's true," Ashley said.

"I just have to *kiss* Conrad, that's all," Mary-Kate said. "But you're cool with that, too, right?"

Kiss?

Ashley froze. Her mouth opened but nothing came out.

"Oh, well, I've got to fly," Mary-Kate said. "My English class starts in five minutes."

Still in shock, Ashley watched her sister run towards the English building.

"Conrad and Kim *kiss*?" Ashley gasped to herself. "No way!"

Ashley's head was spinning. How could Mary-Kate kiss Ross when *she* hadn't even kissed him yet?

"Then again," Ashley muttered to herself as she paced back and forth, "it would be even worse to have Ross kiss Valerie! Then again, Mary-Kate could start to fall in love with Ross during the kissing rehearsals – or the other way around!"

Ashley stopped pacing.

"Then again," she mumbled, "Mary-Kate might be so nervous during the play that she'll kiss badly, which will be even worse because we're twins, and Ross will think that I kiss badly, too! What am I going to doooooo?"

Ashley hurried to her maths lesson. She had decided to keep her mouth shut. The play was important to Mary-Kate and she didn't want to spoil it for her.

If only I had some part in the show – even a teeny weeny one, Ashley thought. *That way I could keep an eye on Mary-Kate and Ross.*

"Not that I don't trust them," Ashley told herself.

Ashley saw a figure racing down the path. She was holding a pile of clothing so high it covered her face. But Ashley knew those white 1960s go-go boots anywhere. It was Phoebe!

"Whoa!" Ashley called out. "Slow down!"

Phoebe peeked over the clothes. "Hi, Ashley," she sighed. "I spent all of the lunch break sewing buttons on these costumes."

"Wow," Ashley said. "I didn't know you had so much work."

Phoebe nodded. "Being the only student in charge of costumes is too huge a job for just one!"

"Really?" Ashley asked slowly.

The wheels in Ashley's head began to spin. If she worked with Phoebe on the costumes, then she could be backstage during rehearsals at all times!

"Phoebe, my pal," Ashley said with a grin. "What you need is an assistant!"

CHAPTER NINE

"Ashley Burke, reporting to fashion duty!" Ashley gave Phoebe a little salute.

It was Monday and Ashley's first day as wardrobe assistant. Phoebe had already given her a tour of the costume warehouse. The huge space outside the Performing Arts Centre was filled with costumes and props from past White Oak plays. The theatre costume room, where they would do all the sewing and fitting, was backstage.

"Now, remember Mrs Tuttle's biggest rule," Phoebe said in a low voice. "The door must be closed whenever we use the sewing machine. It's as noisy as a tank!"

"Got it!" Ashley said. But her eyes weren't on the

clunky grey sewing machine—they were on the door.

Perfect! Ashley thought. *When the door is open I can see the stage. And Ross and Mary-Kate.*

Not that I don't trust them!

"Okay, Ashley!" a gruff voice called out.

Mrs Tuttle! Ashley thought with a groan.

Phoebe had already introduced the White Oak seamstress to Ashley. The tall sewing teacher had charcoal grey hair. She wore pink stretch trousers and a work coat the colour of oatmeal. A measuring tape was draped round her neck and a tomato-shaped pincushion bulged in her pocket.

"You can start by pinning the darts on that bodice," Mrs Tuttle said, pointing to a royal blue dress.

"No problem, Mrs Tuttle," Ashley said. "Except . . . what are darts and what's a bodice?"

Mrs Tuttle peered over her glasses at Ashley. "I had a feeling you never took my Introduction to Sewing class!"

"I'll sew the bodice!" Phoebe cut in. "Ashley can pin a two-inch hem on Kim's poodle skirt."

"Great!" Ashley said as Mrs Tuttle walked away. "Which one is the poodle skirt?"

Phoebe turned Ashley in the direction of a pink

49

skirt. "The one with the big poodle!"

Ashley smiled as she walked to the blue felt skirt with the pink poodle appliqué. She couldn't resist trying it on. Checking to make sure Mrs Tuttle was busy, Ashley slipped the skirt over her jeans and began to spin round.

"There you are!" a girl's voice called out.

Ashley stopping spinning. She saw Valerie Metcalf standing next to a girl with curly blonde hair.

"Meet my roommate, Sybil Walker," Valerie said. "Sybil wants to congratulate you on getting the lead."

Ashley smiled. Valerie thought she was Mary-Kate. She and her sister weren't identical twins, but most people would never know it. "Oh, I'm not—" she began to say.

Sybil shook Ashley's hand. Then she sneezed. "S-sorry," Sybil sniffed. "I've got a wicked cold!"

"Cold?" Ashley grabbed her hand back as Sybil exploded with another sneeze. And another!

"You goofed, Valerie," Ashley said, stepping back. "I'm not Mary-Kate. I'm her twin. Ashley."

"Ashley?" Valerie looked surprised. She grabbed Sybil by the arm and pulled her towards the door. "Let's go, Sybil," she said. "All those germs wasted – on a twin!"

Germs! So that's it, Ashley thought. *Valerie wants*

Mary-Kate to fall ill so she can play the part of Kim!

Ashley slipped out of the poodle skirt. She grabbed a box of pins and got to work.

"Ashley, you've got to see this," Phoebe called excitedly. She ran over and held up a green chiffon dress with tiny spaghetti straps. "This is what Kim is going to wear in the final scene. When she sings *Bye Bye Birdie!*"

"Awesome!" Ashley said, lightly touching the dress.

"And it goes with a matching green bolero jacket," Phoebe said. "All it needs is a pocket and it's all set."

"Um . . . Phoebe?" Ashley asked. "But what is Kim going to wear in the 'One Last Kiss' scene?"

"Oh, that!" Phoebe's eyes glowed. "I thought Kim could wear a simple skirt and sweater. Maybe cashmere."

"Ouch!" Ashley pricked herself with a pin. Did Ross have to kiss Mary-Kate in – cashmere?

"You're not bleeding on that poodle skirt, are you?" Mrs Tuttle barked.

"No, no." Ashley turned to Phoebe. "It's just— are you sure the cashmere sweater is a good choice for Kim?"

"What would *you* suggest?" Phoebe asked.

Ashley ran to a rack filled with costumes.

"Let's see." Ashley yanked out a long black cape with a starched white collar and cap. "As your assistant, may I suggest this? It's understated yet quite elegant."

"It's also the Salvation Army costume we used two years ago in *Guys and Dolls*," Mrs Tuttle said.

"What's up with you, Ashley?" Phoebe asked, annoyed.

Ashley's shoulders dropped. How could she tell Phoebe that she didn't want Mary-Kate to look too good for Ross?

"I must have put too much sugar on my oatmeal this morning." Ashley sighed. "I don't know what's the matter with me!"

"Forget it," Phoebe whispered. "Now, let's get to work before Mrs Tuttle has a major meltdown."

Hanging up the black cape, Ashley began to worry.

Was Mary-Kate right? Ashley wondered. *Am I really beginning to mistrust my own twin sister?*

CHAPTER TEN

"I can't believe the play is only a week away!" Mary-Kate said, sitting in her biology lesson.

It was a few minutes past eleven o'clock. The pupils were waiting for their teacher to arrive.

"You know what that means!" Summer giggled. "You're a week away from kissing one of the biggest hunks at Harrington!"

Mary-Kate felt herself blush. It had been a few days since she had set the record straight with Ashley. But that didn't make her less nervous about kissing Ross!

"I kissed a boy once!" Elise blurted.

"What was it like?" Summer asked.

"The pits," Elise admitted. "I wore braces and so

53

did he. We were in a jaw lock for almost an hour."

"Ouch!" Summer said.

"Girlfriends, I'll kiss a boy when I'm good and ready," Cheryl said firmly. She turned to Mary-Kate. "Hey, Mary-Kate, isn't Ross the guy that Ashley likes?"

Mary-Kate nodded. "I guess you can say that."

"Then didn't she have a fit when you told her about the smooch?" Cheryl asked.

"Ashley was cool," Mary-Kate said honestly. "Besides, Ross and I will just be acting out the parts of Kim and Conrad. It's not as if we feel anything for each other."

"Then it's *not* acting!" a voice behind Mary-Kate declared. Mary-Kate rolled her eyes. She knew that voice anywhere. It was Valerie Metcalf!

Mary-Kate turned around slowly. Valerie was wearing a lavender sweater today—with pink and white feathers!

"What do you mean, it's not acting?" Mary-Kate asked.

"I mean that according to the famous Stanislavsky method acting," Valerie said, "an actor must not just play a part. He or she must *feel* the part!"

"Give me a break," Cheryl muttered.

"So if I were playing Kim," Valerie wrapped her arms round her shoulders and smiled, "I'd make sure I fell in love with Ross Lambert. And really enjoyed that kiss!"

Valerie flipped her hair and walked back to her microscope.

"Who does she think she is, telling you how to act, Mary-Kate?" Cheryl asked.

Mary-Kate forced herself to smile. "It's okay, you guys," she said. "I don't take anything that Valerie says seriously."

But deep inside, Mary-Kate knew that wasn't totally true. Maybe Valerie was right in a crazy way. Maybe she was having trouble with the kissing scene because she wasn't in love with Ross Lambert!

But how could she force herself to have a crush on a boy she just liked as a friend?

As her teacher walked into the classroom, Mary-Kate had a horrible thought:

Maybe I'm not such a great actress, after all. Maybe I should just stick to softball.

"Mary-Kate?" Campbell called in to the shower room. "Mary-Kate – are you in here?"

Mary-Kate rubbed the strawberry-scented

shampoo through her wet hair. She couldn't see Campbell through the shower curtain. But her voice sounded urgent!

"What's up?" Mary-Kate called through the water.

"Thank goodness I found you!" Campbell breathed a sigh of relief. "You're supposed to be rehearsing the 'How Lovely to Be a Woman' song right now. Mr Boulderblatt is raving mad!"

Mary-Kate peeked out of the shower with suds on her head. "The schedule said my call wasn't until eight o'clock tonight. That's why I spent all afternoon practising my pitching."

"Practise your *running*," Campbell said. "Mr Boulderblatt wanted you at the theatre twenty minutes ago!"

"Great!" Mary-Kate groaned. She was sure she had read eight o'clock on the schedule. Positive!

After rinsing and pulling on her grey tracksuit, Mary-Kate and Campbell ran out of the shower room and into the hall. They stopped in front of the rehearsal schedule hanging on the Porter House notice board.

"You see?" Mary-Kate cried. She jabbed a dripping wet finger at the schedule. "Mary-Kate Burke, eight p.m. Not five p.m!"

"Unless . . ." Campbell moved closer to the notice board and squinted. "Someone turned the five into an eight!"

Mary-Kate practically pressed her nose against the schedule. She could see what Campbell meant – the number eight did look a bit square at the top!

"Why would someone change it?" Mary-Kate asked.

"*Who* would change it?" Campbell added.

"I don't have a clue," Mary-Kate said, yanking the schedule from the notice board. "I just know I have to get to rehearsal—fast!"

A sopping-wet Mary-Kate left puddles on the concrete as she ran with Campbell to the Performing Arts Centre. Out of breath, Mary-Kate burst into the theatre with Campbell right behind her.

"Sorry I'm—" Mary-Kate started to say. But when she glanced at the stage she froze. Valerie was dancing around Kim's bedroom set and singing "How Lovely to Be a Woman"!

"Excuse me!" Mary-Kate shouted out.

Perry stopped playing the piano. Mr Boulderblatt turned round and stared at Mary-Kate.

"Well! There you are, Mary-Kate!" Mr

Boulderblatt said. "How good of you to drop by!"

"You mean *drip* by!" Valerie sneered.

Valerie! Mary-Kate thought angrily. *It was Valerie who changed my schedule!*

"What is she doing?" Mary-Kate asked, pointing at Valerie. "Why is she singing my song?"

"You know the rules, Mary-Kate," Mr Boulderblatt said. "If you don't show up for rehearsal without a solid excuse, you're out of the show."

"But Mary-Kate *does* have an excuse!" Campbell said. She gave Mary-Kate a nudge. "Show him, Mary-Kate."

"Someone changed the five o'clock to eight o'clock," Mary-Kate held up the schedule and glared at Valerie. "And I think I know who!"

"It's the classic case of the eager understudy, Mr Boulderblatt!" Campbell declared.

"Oh, pleeeease! Pleeeease!" Mr Boulderblatt said, rolling his eyes. "I'm a director—not Nancy Drew!"

"So you see, Mr Boulderblatt, it wasn't my fault!" Mary-Kate went on.

"Okay, okay, Mary-Kate!" Mr Boulderblatt sighed. "Let's rehearse your number."

"Yes!" Mary-Kate cheered under her breath. She could see Valerie pouting on the stage.

"What about me?" Valerie demanded. "My voice is better than hers! And my hair looks better in a ponytail, too!"

"Thank you, Valerie," Mr Boulderblatt said. "When we need you, we'll call you."

Valerie's ponytail almost whipped Mary-Kate in the face as she whirled around and marched out of the theatre.

"I'd watch out for her if I were you, Mary-Kate," Campbell said as the two walked to the dressing room.

"What else can Valerie do?" Mary-Kate asked. "Plant banana peels outside my door? Drop a sandbag on my head?"

"Knowing Valerie, it's possible," Campbell said.

"No it's not!" Mary-Kate insisted. "Campbell, I'm going to play Kim even if I have to act in a body cast!"

CHAPTER ELEVEN

"How are you coming along on that pocket, Ashley?" Mrs Tuttle called from the sewing machine. "The show is tomorrow, you know. And that green bolero jacket is for the final number."

"Just about done!" Ashley called back from behind a dressing screen. "I just have to . . . tie the finishing knot!"

Ashley patted the pocket in place. She hoped no one would see that she used double-stick tape to "sew" the pocket on to the jacket. "There!" she said to herself.

Not that Ashley didn't *try* to sew the pocket. But after days of tangled threads and needle jabs, there had to be another way.

"Done!" Ashley said, coming out from behind the screen. She held the jacket and her breath as Mrs Tuttle glanced up from the sewing machine.

"Looks good," Mrs Tuttle said, tilting her head. "For three days' worth of work!"

"Ashley likes to be thorough," Phoebe said. She grinned at Ashley as she pinned the hem on Tatiana Riccio's dress. "And a stitch in time saves nine!"

Except I didn't use any stitches, Ashley thought.

She draped the green bolero jacket over the chiffon dress. Then she hung a tag over the hanger with Mary-Kate's name and scene number.

Ashley took a deep breath. Most of the costumes were selected, pulled, fitted and tagged. She and Phoebe had been superbusy over the past few days. So busy that Ashley didn't even have a moment to think about Ross!

Ashley smiled when she heard Perry play the first chords of her favourite number, "The Telephone Hour". Running to the door, Ashley peeked out at the stage.

Wendy, Campbell, Summer, Kristen and Aaron Meltzer, who was playing Harvey Johnson, were sitting on big comfy pillows. They were holding colourful telephones and kicking their feet in the air.

A few other cast members watched from the wings. One of them was their cousin Jeremy.

"Have you heard about Hugo and Kim?" Summer sang. "Did they really get— ow!"

"What is the matter, now, Summer?" Mr Boulderblatt asked when Perry stopped playing.

"I got my finger stuck in this humongous telephone!" Summer whined.

Mr Boulderblatt waved his arms in the air. "I can't understand why you kids are having so much trouble handling those phones!" he said.

"For one," Kristen said, "we're not used to phones with these stupid wheels on them."

"I will repeat it for the tenth time," Mr Boulderblatt said slowly. "Years ago telephones were dialled, not punched. And they were too big to carry in handbags!"

"Then what good were they?" Summer cried.

Ashley giggled. She was still disappointed that she didn't have a part. But watching from backstage was almost as much fun!

"Burke!" Mrs Tuttle bellowed. "There's a pair of pedal pushers on the ironing board that needs pressing!"

"Sure, Mrs Tuttle." Ashley jumped and hurried over to the ironing board.

I suppose all the costumes aren't ready, Ashley thought as she glided the iron across the bright purple pedal pushers. From where she was standing, she could still hear the rehearsal loud and clear.

"That was much better," Mr Boulderblatt said when the song was over. "Just remember not to kick the person next to you when you're swinging your legs!"

"Are we running through it again?" Campbell asked.

"No," Mr Boulderblatt said. "We'll run through all the songs tomorrow at the dress rehearsal. The scenes, too."

"Even the kissing scene?" Jeremy laughed.

"Yes, Jeremy, even the kissing scene!" Mr Boulderblatt replied.

Ashley glanced up from her ironing. She gulped as she heard Jeremy make sloppy kissing noises.

Oh, no! I was so busy that I completely forgot about the kiss! Ashley thought in a panic. *I can't let Mary-Kate kiss Ross before I do – I just can't!*

Suddenly Phoebe let out a shriek.

"Ashley!" she cried. "You're burning the pedal pushers!"

CHAPTER TWELVE

"They should call this the *stress* rehearsal!" Ashley joked as she helped Mary-Kate button her cashmere cardigan.

"Stress rehearsal?" Mary-Kate repeated.

"That was a joke – hel-lo?" Ashley said.

"Oh! Cute!" Mary-Kate forced herself to laugh. "Dress, stress. I get it."

But Mary-Kate didn't really feel like laughing. All she could think about was the scene they were going to rehearse. The scene where Conrad Birdie kissed Kim McAfee.

"The 'One Last Kiss' number begins in three minutes!" Mr Boulderblatt called. "Three minutes!"

"One Last Kiss", Mary-Kate thought. *This is it.*

"Mary-Kate, you're trembling!" Ashley said. "You weren't trembling before!"

"It's chilly back here," Mary-Kate lied. How could she tell Ashley that she was nervous about the kiss scene? Especially after they had decided it was no big deal.

It wasn't . . . was it?

Maybe she had better make sure.

"Ashley?" Mary-Kate said slowly. "You still don't mind that I'm kissing Ross, do you?"

"No way!" Ashley brushed Mary-Kate's skirt with a lint brush. "As they say in the song – a kiss is just a kiss!"

If only I could feel that way! Mary-Kate thought.

She gave a little jump when Perry played the introduction to the scene. Jeremy ran past her.

"Where's Ross?" Mary-Kate could hear Mr Boulderblatt calling. "Get Ross Lambert!"

"Cool your jets, Daddio! I'm coming!"

Mary-Kate saw Ross strut by in a tight gold jumpsuit and boots. A guitar rested on his shoulder.

"Doesn't he look cute?" Ashley whispered.

Mary-Kate gulped. She still didn't have a crush on Ross. But she had to admit – in a get-up like that he did look pretty hot!

"Good luck, Mary-Kate!" Ashley said.

Mary-Kate nodded at her sister. Then she walked to the wings. Peeking out, she could see Valerie sitting in the first row. Her legs were crossed, and she was coolly filing her nails.

Forget about her, Mary-Kate thought as she joined Ross and Jeremy on stage. *Just concentrate on your scene – and get it over with!*

Mr Boulderblatt nodded at Jeremy to say his line.

Jeremy crossed his arms and hunched up his shoulders. "And now a treat for all you youngsters," Jeremy as Ed Sullivan announced. "Let's hear it for – Conrad Birdie!"

Ross turned to Mary-Kate. Swinging his hips and strumming his guitar, he began to sing, "One Last Kiss."

Mary-Kate tried to appear starry-eyed. When the song was over, she recited her little speech to Conrad. Then it was time for the kiss.

Mary-Kate held her breath as Ross leaned over. But just as he began to pucker up—

"Stop!" Ashley shouted.

Mary-Kate froze.

"I have to take Kim's measurements right now!" Ashley said as she ran to Mary-Kate with a measuring tape.

"Now?" Mr Boulderblatt cried. "During a dress rehearsal?"

"Her bolero jacket might be too tight!" Ashley told Mr Boulderblatt. She swung the measuring tape like a lasso around Mary-Kate.

"Forget it, Ashley," Mary-Kate said, annoyed. "Mrs Tuttle already took my measurements, remember?"

"That was days ago. Before you had that hot fudge sundae with the extra nuts!" Ashley said. "You'd be surprised what hot fudge does for the waistline!"

"This is too much!" Ross chuckled.

From the corner of her eye Mary-Kate could see Phoebe coming to her rescue.

"Ashley," Phoebe said, grabbing Ashley's arm. "Mrs Tuttle left to get coffee and I have to find some coloured chalk. Can you please watch the costume room while I'm gone?"

"Yes, Ashley," Mr Boulderblatt growled. "Watch the costume room. Pleeeeeease?"

"Okay," Ashley said, taking back the measuring tape. "No problem."

Mary-Kate noticed that Ashley's eyes were on Ross as she walked away with Phoebe.

Wait a minute! Mary-Kate thought. *Ashley said she*

didn't care about the kiss. So what's up?

"Now, let's try this again," Mr Boulderblatt groaned. "Conrad is about to kiss Kim. Take it from the pucker."

Here goes, Mary-Kate thought as Ross leaned over to kiss her. *Should I keep my eyes open or closed? Should I move closer to him or do I wait until he moves closer to me? Did I remember to take my gum out?*

But just as Ross's and Mary-Kate's lips were about to meet—

WHIIIIIIRRRRRRRRRR!

Mary-Kate and Ross clapped their hands over their ears.

"It's that blasted sewing machine!" Mr Boulderblatt cried, throwing his script on the floor.

Everyone turned towards the costume room. Ashley slowly poked her head out of the door and smiled. "Sorry," she squeaked.

Mary-Kate groaned with everyone else. Ashley had interrupted the kissing scene again!

"Hmmm," Valerie said, studying her nails. "Looks like this scene isn't working out."

Mary-Kate wondered what was going on. Ashley was trying to prevent their kiss – after she said it was no big deal! What did Ashley really think?

"You have interrupted this scene for the last

time, Ashley!" Mr Boulderblatt warned.

"I'm sorry, Mr Boulderblatt," Ashley said. "It won't happen again."

Mr Boulderblatt ran his hand through his hair and sighed. "Let's take a fifteen-minute break," he announced. "When we come back, we'll pick up the scene *after* the kiss."

After the kiss?

Mary-Kate heaved a sigh of relief. Now she and Ross wouldn't have to rehearse the kiss at all. They would do it once during the play and that would be that!

"Aw, nuts," Jeremy said, walking away. "This I wanted to see!"

Ross turned to Mary-Kate and smiled. "Oh, well," he said. "Want to grab a Coke or something?"

"No, thanks, Ross." Mary-Kate glared at Ashley. "There's something I have to take care of first."

Mary-Kate was annoyed with Ashley. Not for interrupting the kiss – but for not being honest with her.

And from the look on Ashley's face before she ducked back into the costume room, she knew she was in trouble!

CHAPTER THIRTEEN

"Uh-oh," Ashley said to herself when she saw Mary-Kate glare at her. "Better run."

Ashley turned on her heel. She raced out of the back door towards the costume warehouse.

Mary-Kate will never find me there, Ashley thought. *That place is a mess.*

But once inside the warehouse, Ashley hid behind a dress with a huge hoop skirt.

"Hey, Ashley?" Mary-Kate called as the door creaked open. "You in here? Come out, come out, wherever you are!"

Ashley clutched the skirt. Then she let out a loud yelp. A pin inside the hem stuck her finger!

"Busted!" Mary-Kate cried as she pulled aside

the hoop skirt. "Okay, Ashley," she said, folding her arms across her chest. "What's the deal?"

Ashley sighed. There was no use denying it anymore. "Look, Mary-Kate," she said. "I didn't think I'd react that way. But every time Ross was about to kiss you, something strange came over me. I just couldn't let you and Ross kiss. Not when I haven't even kissed him yet."

Mary-Kate smiled weakly. "Can I make a confession?" she asked.

"What?" Ashley was afraid to ask. *Was Mary-Kate going to say that she liked Ross, too?*

"I don't even *want* to kiss Ross," Mary-Kate said.

"You don't?" Ashley asked a little too excitedly.

"It's my least favourite scene," Mary-Kate admitted. "I've never kissed a boy in front of hundreds of people."

"I've never kissed a boy period!" Ashley said.

The twins sat down on a giant fake toadstool.

"You know, if only there was a way I could kiss Ross for you," Ashley joked. "Everyone's always saying how much we look alike. Even Valerie!"

Mary-Kate raised her eyebrows in a high arch.

"Hey!" she said. "Let's do it, Ashley!"

"Mary-Kate, I was just joking!" Ashley cried.

"I'm not," Mary-Kate said. "Kim has just a tiny

little speech which you can learn by tomorrow. As for the costume, I have my own dressing room, remember?"

Ashley nodded. But she still couldn't believe her sister was serious!

"All you have to do is put on this skirt and sweater," Mary-Kate said. "Then go out, kiss Ross, and run back!"

Ashley stood up and paced the floor. She imagined herself in the spotlight – kissing Ross Lambert – the boy of her dreams.

"Well?" Mary-Kate asked, jumping up from the toadstool. "What do you say?"

Ashley stopped pacing. She turned to Mary-Kate with a serious look on her face. Then she smiled slowly.

"You've always had a lot of schemes," Ashley said. "But this is the most brilliant scheme you've ever had!"

Ashley gave Mary-Kate a high five.

Their plan was in place. Now all they had to do was pull it off!

CHAPTER FOURTEEN

"On behalf of all members of the Sweet Apple Conrad Birdie Fan Club . . ." Ashley recited in Mary-Kate's dressing room the next evening. "On behalf of all members—"

"Not again!" Mary-Kate groaned. "You'll be fine, Ashley. And your scene isn't until the end."

"I think I'm as nervous as you are," Ashley sighed.

"Do you have to remind me?" Mary-Kate cried. She pressed her ear to the door. Even though her dressing room was down the hall from the stage, she could hear the excitement as the cast and crew scurried backstage and hundreds of students and guests filed into the Performing Arts Centre. It was opening night at White Oak Academy!

"Let's go over our switch again," Ashley said. "I want to make sure I get it right."

"Okay," Mary-Kate said. "During Albert and Rosie's scene, we'll both run in here. Then you'll put on Kim's costume for the 'One Last Kiss' number."

"The pink skirt and cashmere sweater!" Ashley added. "Got it!"

"Then," Mary-Kate went on, "when the kissing scene begins, you run out, say your line, and kiss Ross. I'll stay here and change into the costume for my final 'Bye Bye Birdie' number."

"The green chiffon dress with matching bolero jacket!" Ashley added. "Got it!"

Mary-Kate nodded. "As soon as the curtain goes down, you run back here and I'll run back out to sing 'Bye Bye Birdie'. Do you know the drill?"

Ashley nodded. Then she looked at the clock and gasped. "Oh, no! I have to help the Conrad Birdie Fan Club with their ponytails!" she cried.

"Remember!" Mary-Kate said as Ashley slipped out of the door. "After your scene get right back here so I can be Kim again."

The door slammed shut. Alone in her dressing room, Mary-Kate began to have second thoughts.

What if someone finds out about our big switch? What if Mrs Pritchard finds out? What was I thinking?

Mary-Kate heard a knock on the door.

"W-w-who is it?" Mary-Kate stammered.

"It's Mrs Pritchard!"

Mary-Kate bit her lip hard. Had the Head already find out about their plan?

Opening the door slowly, Mary-Kate peeked out. "Yes, Mrs Pritchard?"

"Surprise!" Mrs Pritchard held up a colourful flower arrangement and a box of chocolates. "A bouquet from your father in Chicago. With love!"

Mary-Kate smiled with relief. She flung the door wide open and took the bouquet from Mrs Pritchard.

"My dad's the greatest!" Mary-Kate said. "Thanks, Mrs Pritchard!"

"There's a card, too, Mary-Kate!" Mrs Pritchard pointed out. "Why don't you read it?"

Pulling out the small white card, Mary-Kate read it to herself:

Dear Mary-Kate: I am so proud of my leading lady! I know you'll do a great job. Love, Dad
P. S. Share the chocolates with your sister!

Mary-Kate gulped. That wasn't all she'd be sharing with her sister tonight!

CHAPTER FIFTEEN

"So far so good!" Sara-Beth Ang, the girl in charge of the curtain, whispered to Ashley and Phoebe.

Ashley showed Sara-Beth that her fingers were crossed. So far the musical had gone without a hitch. No one had lost their costumes or forgotten their lines. Except for a squeaky garden swing in the "One Boy" number, and a couple of girls complaining about tight ponytails, *Bye Bye Birdie* was turning out to be a hit!

"What is Rosie wearing in the next number?" Phoebe whispered to Ashley.

"She's wearing the blue kiss—" Ashley blurted. "I mean – dress!"

Ashley wanted to slap her forehead. As busy as

she was, she still couldn't keep her mind off the big switch.

"I forgot," Phoebe said. "Does Rosie's blue dress go with the pearl choker or the butterfly pin?"

"Neither," Ashley said. "It goes with the silver smooch—"

"Smooch?" Phoebe asked.

Ashley felt her cheeks burn. "I mean – brooch!"

"Ashley, I know we've been working hard, but are you okay?" Phoebe asked.

"I'm fine!" Ashley chirped. "Couldn't be better!"

"Good," Phoebe whispered. "Because Mr Boulderblatt is coming this way. Look busy!"

Ashley grabbed Summer Sorenson and began retying her ponytail. Phoebe brushed lint off Summer's sweater.

"Hey! My scene is over!" Summer protested.

"Ashley, Phoebe," Mr Boulderblatt said. "We're going to start getting ready for the 'One Last Kiss' number."

"Ouch!" Summer cried as Ashley accidentally yanked her ponytail.

"Sorry!" Ashley told Summer. She turned to Phoebe. "I need some water first. I'll be right back!"

Ashley turned on her heel and ran down the hall to Mary-Kate's dressing room.

"Mary-Kate, open up!" Ashley said, knocking on the door. "It's time for the 'One Last Kiss' scene!"

Mary-Kate opened the door. She shoved the cashmere sweater and skirt into Ashley's arms. "Make it snappy!"

Ashley hurried into the dressing room, shut the door, and quickly changed into the outfit.

"Cashmere!" Ashley swooned as she ran her hands along her sleeves. "Cashmeeeeere!"

"I'm glad *you* like it," Mary-Kate said. "It makes me itch like a dog with fleas!"

A knock on the door made the twins jump.

"Five minutes, Mary-Kate!" Chris Hernandez, the stage manager, called through the door. "Five minutes!"

"Thanks, Chris!" Mary-Kate called back. She turned to Ashley. "What are you waiting for? That means you!"

Ashley froze as it suddenly hit her.

"Me?" she squeaked. "You mean I have to go on stage? In front of all those people?"

"You're on!" Mary-Kate said. She opened the door and shoved Ashley into the hall.

"Wait!" Ashley said. "I want to rehearse my—"

The door slammed shut.

"Speech!" Ashley finished.

She leaned against the door and took a deep breath. Her heart was pounding inside her chest. Sweat was beginning to bead on her forehead.

Maybe I should wait another *twelve years before I kiss a boy*, Ashley thought.

"Mary-Kate!" Phoebe came running over. "Oh, good! You have on your skirt and cashmere sweater!"

Mary-Kate! Ashley thought. She quickly shoved her silver butterfly necklace under her sweater. *That's me now!*

"Yes, and this cashmere feels so good!" Ashley said.

"That's funny," Phoebe said. "I thought it made you itch like a dog."

Ashley gulped. "Yes!" she blurted. "I mean – it feels so good when I take the stupid thing off!"

"Whatever," Phoebe said. "Just don't be late for your big scene."

"My scene!" Ashley gasped. She shoved Phoebe aside and ran all the way backstage. Her heart fluttered as Ross walked over in his tight gold jumpsuit.

"Good luck!" Ross whispered as the curtain rose.

Ashley tried not to look at the audience. But she could feel the hundreds of eyes planted right on her!

After Jeremy said his line, Ross began to sing. "One last kiss . . ."

79

When Ross gave his guitar one final strum, she saw Mr Boulderblatt signal to her from the wings.

My speech! Ashley thought. She cleared her throat and threw back her shoulders.

"O-on behalf of all members of the Sweet Apple Conrad Birdie Fan Club," Ashley said. "We wish to express our deep pride in your brave deed."

Ross handed his guitar to Jeremy. Then he leaned over and locked lips with Ashley.

Bells! Fireworks!

Although her eyes were squeezed shut, Ashley could feel her eyeballs spinning behind her fluttering lids.

Ashley's head was definitely in the clouds. So much that when Hugo came to break it up, she couldn't do it!

"Cut it, will you?" Jeremy hissed.

Ashley let go and stumbled back. Ross's eyes were huge and his mouth hung open.

The scene continued all around Ashley but all she could think was . . .

I kissed Ross! I finally kissed Ross Lambert!

As for Mary-Kate, her head was *not* in the clouds. It was spinning as she searched frantically for the green chiffon dress with matching bolero jacket.

"Where is it?" Mary-Kate wondered out loud as she dug through her costume rack. "Where did it go?"

Mary-Kate heard the faint sound of applause. In just a few seconds she would have to go out and sing her final number. But she couldn't sing it without her green chiffon dress and bolero jacket!

"What am I going to do?" Mary-Kate groaned.

She was about to pull all the clothes off the rack, when she heard a loud *CLICK*.

Mary-Kate froze. It came from her dressing-room door.

"Is somebody out there?" Mary-Kate called as she moved toward the door. "Ashley? Is that you?"

But when Mary-Kate tried to twist the doorknob, it wouldn't turn.

The door was locked!

Mary-Kate ran to the dresser and opened the top drawer. Not only was the door locked – but the key was gone, too!

Oh, great! Mary-Kate thought. *Someone's locked me inside my own dressing room!*

CHAPTER
SIXTEEN

Ashley was still grinning as the curtain came down. She didn't notice the other players and stagehands rushing around her and getting ready for the final scene.

"Mary-Kate!"

Ashley looked up. Ross was coming her way.

"Yes, Ross?" Ashley asked sweetly.

"That kiss," Ross said. "It was uh . . . really convincing. But I guess that's what makes you such a good actress, Mary-Kate!"

"Mary-Kate." Ashley chuckled to herself. She smiled up at Ross. "Ross, do you promise to keep a huge secret?"

"I suppose so." Ross shrugged.

"That Kim you were kissing was not Mary-Kate," Ashley said excitedly. She pulled the silver butterfly necklace from her sweater. "It was me – Ashley!"

"Ashley?" Ross stared at the butterfly necklace, then at Ashley. "Wow!"

"Mary-Kate!" Mr Boulderblatt called as he hurried over with Phoebe. "Why are you hanging around back here? You should be getting ready for your big number."

"And changing into your green chiffon dress with matching bolero jacket!" Phoebe added.

Ashley stiffened. She was so busy switching with Mary-Kate that she forgot all about switching back!

"I'm going, I'm going," Ashley said. "I'll see you later," she whispered to Ross. He still looked stunned.

Ashley ran straight to Mary-Kate's dressing room. She knocked on the door.

"Open up!" Ashley called.

"I can't!" Mary-Kate called back.

"What do you mean, you can't?" Ashley demanded.

"Someone locked me in here!" Mary-Kate said.

Ashley stepped back from the door. "They can't do that – you're the star of the show!" she cried.

"I'm telling Mr Boulderblatt!"

"Hel-lo?" Mary-Kate said. "If you tell Mr Boulderblatt then he'll know that we switched. We can't tell *anyone*!"

"Then what are we going to do?" Ashley asked.

"I don't know," Mary-Kate said. "But how well can you sing, 'Bye Bye Birdie'?"

"What?" Ashley gasped. She leaned against the door and squeezed her eyes shut. "Oh, noooooo!"

Ashley's eyes were still closed when she heard Summer's voice around the hall corner.

"No way!" Summer was saying. "I can't believe you're taking over the lead, Valerie!"

Valerie? Lead?

Ashley's eyes popped open.

"Poor Mary-Kate isn't feeling well," Valerie sighed. "So I guess I'll be going in as an understudy – and coming out a star!"

Turning her head, Ashley could see Valerie coming around the corner. She was dressed in the green chiffon dress with matching bolero jacket!

So that's who locked Mary-Kate in the dressing room, Ashley thought. *Valerie Metcalf – the understudy!*

CHAPTER SEVENTEEN

"Nice dress!" Ashley said, stepping in front of Valerie. "Where did you get it?"

Valerie froze when she saw Ashley.

"What are you doing out here?" she demanded. "You should be locked in your dressing room. I mean—"

"You *did* lock me in, Valerie!" Mary-Kate's muffled voice called through the door.

Valerie stared at the door, then at Ashley. "You did it again!" she complained. "I still can't tell you apart!"

"Here's a way," Ashley said, grinning. "I'm the one who knows karate. Now give me the key!"

Ashley didn't really know karate.

But it sure sounded good!

"Um," Summer said nervously. "I've got to run. And brush up on my . . . curtain call!"

Summer ran away and Ashley turned back to Valerie.

"Well?" Ashley held out her hand. "Give me the key!"

"Yeah!" Mary-Kate's voice called. "Give her the key!"

Valerie stuck out her chin. Then she placed her hand over the pocket of her bolero jacket.

Ashley could see the faint outline of a key through the material.

"If you want to play Kim so badly," Valerie told Ashley. "Then why don't you sing her final number, too?"

Final number?

Ashley felt sick. She didn't know the words to "Bye Bye Birdie". She even sang "Happy Birthday" off-key!

I have to free Mary-Kate, Ashley thought, narrowing her eyes. *If it's the last thing I do!*

Staring at the pocket, Ashley remembered the double-stick tape. The pocket wasn't sewn on – it was stuck on!

Reaching out, Ashley grabbed the pocket. Then

with one quick rip she tore the pocket right off.

"Hey!" Valerie complained as the key dropped.

"I never did like that pocket," Ashley said, snatching up the key.

Ashley quickly unlocked the door. Mary-Kate burst out of her dressing room and marched straight to Valerie.

"If you want to stay here at White Oak you'll give me back my dress!" Mary-Kate demanded.

Ashley stood next to Mary-Kate and crossed her arms. "It's two against one, Valerie. Do the maths."

Valerie's perfectly pencilled eyebrows shot up as she stared at Mary-Kate and Ashley. She seemed to know that the Burkes meant business!

"Okay, okay!" Valerie sighed. "I shouldn't have taken your dress. It's just that I wanted to be in the show so badly that the final number was my last-ditch effort!"

"So you broke into my dressing room?" Mary-Kate asked.

"The door was open," Valerie insisted. "So I sneaked in this morning and took the green dress and jacket."

Ashley felt awful. She had been so busy worrying about the kiss that she hadn't noticed the dress was missing.

"Hey, look, I promise to keep your secret if you keep mine," Valerie said. "Okay?"

Ashley studied Valerie. She looked worried – and this time she wasn't acting!

"Mary-Kate!" Chris called down the hall. "Five minutes to the 'Bye Bye Birdie' number!"

"Five minutes?" Mary-Kate gasped. She turned to Valerie. "Okay. It's a deal!"

Valerie ran into the dressing room. The three did a quick change – Valerie out of the dress, Mary-Kate into the dress, and Ashley back into her regular clothes.

"What about the pocket?" Mary-Kate asked as she slipped into the jacket.

"No problem!" Ashley said. She grinned as she stuck the pocket back in place.

In a flash the twins ran backstage. The curtain was just about to go up on Mary-Kate's final number.

"There you are!" Phoebe said as she scurried past Ashley. "We have a fashion emergency. Becky Lapinski has a rash from her petticoat, and Tommy Mateo's tight jeans just split!"

"I'll be right there!" Ashley called back. She turned to Mary-Kate and smiled. "Hey. Break a leg!"

"The last time I did that I fell off my bike," Mary-Kate joked.

Ashley giggled. Her sister knew that "break a leg" meant "good luck" in the theatre.

The curtain came up as Perry played the fanfare. Ashley watched as her sister walked into the spotlight and began to sing:

"Bye Bye Birdie! The army's got you now . . . "

Ashley's heart soared as she watched her sister belting out the most important song in the show. Everything had turned out just perfectly. Mary-Kate got to star in a big school musical, and Ashley got to kiss the boy of her dreams.

And there was a huge box of chocolates from their dad waiting in the dressing room!

"I guess it's true what they say," Ashley told herself with a grin. "There's no business like show business!"

ACORN

The Voice of White Oak Academy Since 1905

HOME FOR THE HOLIDAYS!
by Phoebe Cahill

It may be weeks before we trim the tree and light the Advent candle. But White Oakers already have visions of winter break dancing through their heads. How are fellow First Formers planning to spend three awesome weeks of total freedom? In more ways than one ...

When Campbell Smith goes home to Minnesota (brr!) she'll practise her pitching ... with snowballs! Summer Sorenson plans to work on her "fading" tan when she flies home to sunny Malibu, California. Let's hope Summer has a great time and remembers one word: SUNSCREEN!

Way to go, Cheryl Miller! This will be her second winter volunteering at a St Louis animal shelter. Cheryl hopes to raise awareness about stray cats and dogs. And speaking of volunteering, Elise Van

Hook will be visiting her Peace Corps parents in Fiji! Elise can't wait to hang out with the Fiji kids . . . and hang out glitter ornaments on her Christmas palm tree!

Everyone's favourite understudy, Valerie Metcalf, says she'll audition for a major Hollywood motion picture. And if she doesn't get *that* part – there's always another Cornflakes advert!

After Mary-Kate and Ashley Burke recover from final exams they plan to spend quality time with their dad and Chicago pals. They also plan to sleep late, ice skate daily and eat anything for breakfast but oatmeal. Even if it means their dad's rhubarb muffins! As for me, I'm hoping to write a slew of poetry and scan my favourite San Francisco

vintage shops for that perfect mustard-coloured 70s vinyl jacket with wide lapels . . .

Unless I happen to find one under my tree!

GLAM GAB
by Ashley and Phoebe

Fashion expert Ashley Burke

Glam Gab isn't just about fashion. It's about looking good – all year round. Take your room, for instance. Your room is a reflection of you – your tastes, your personality, your interests. We've been looking for some cool ideas on room decorating – and we've found them. Here are some ways to perk up your room – and your life!

1) **Pot Luck.** Get some flower pots – terracotta are the best – and paint them. Go wild with stripes, polka dots, curlicues, whatever – the brighter, the better. You can plant the pots with actual indoor plants (if you don't have green fingers, you might want to grow a miniature cactus – it hardly ever

needs water). Or you can use them to hold pens, pencils, and other useful stuff. Then place the pots on your windowsill – and watch spring bloom!

2) **Flower Power.** Buy some fake flowers (you can get them really cheaply at a discount store) and turn your room into a garden. You can glue the flowers around mirrors, door frames, and windows. For a special touch, glue flowers onto plain lampshades – and your room will glow with all the colours of the rainbow!

3) **Magic Lights.** Hang strands of twinkling lights on your walls. You'll feel as if you're living in a fairy tale!

4) **Picture Perfect.** Paint an old picture frame. Then glue on buttons, sequins, flowers, or feathers. You'll have your own custom-made frame – for your favourite photograph!

AUDIENCE FLOCKS TO SEE *BYE BYE BIRDIE*!
by Mary-Kate "Kim" Burke

We did it! White Oak Academy and Harrington

*Musical comedy star
Mary-Kate Burke*

School performed a major Broadway musical without a hitch!

But success never comes without hard work. So on behalf of the cast of *Bye Bye Birdie*, I'd like to say thanks to everyone who worked on the production – especially Mrs Tuttle and Phoebe Cahill, who put together a totally authentic 1960s wardrobe! I just hope Phoebe plans to leave the clothes in the costume room and not wear them! (Just kidding, Phoeb!)

But we could never have pulled it off without the help of Mr Boulderblatt. He came all the way from Broadway to direct our play and made us all feel like stars. So bye-bye, Mr Boulderblatt. You'll be missed!

BYE BYE,
BIRDIE

As for me, playing Kim was a moment I'll never forget. And about the famous kissing scene . . . well, it happened so fast, I feel like I never even kissed Ross Lambert! And that's the HONEST SINCERE truth!

THE GET-REAL GIRL

Dear Get-Real Girl,

It's my first year at White Oak and I'm really digging it. But I can't stop thinking about my family, my mates back home, even my dog Buster! Is there a cure for homesickness – or should I just get over it?

Signed,
Incurably Homesick

Dear Homesick,

Like the girl with the red shoes in Oz said, there's no place like home. But there are ways to make you feel as if you never left Kansas:

1) Make a tape of your bro-ther nagging you for com-puter time. 2) Wear the new platform sandals that Buster chewed up. 3) Swallow all the vegetables your mum makes you eat. And last but not least, re-member that home may be where the heart is, but White Oak is where good times rule!

Signed,
Get-Real Girl

Dear Get-Real Girl,
My roommate and I get along great. There's only one problem – she has more friends than leopards have spots! And they do all these neat things together, like play paint-ball, go to the cinema and pig out on ice-cream sundaes. But they never invite me! Should I say something – or just bite my tongue?

Signed,
Dejected, Neglected
and Rejected

Dear Dejected,

OUCH! Don't bite your tongue – you're going to need it to eat all those ice-cream sundaes. Because you are going to kick up your courage and tell your roomie that you'd love to be included. If she says "yes", then your troubles are over. If she says "no", forget Miss Popularity and find your own crew to hang out with. And learn how to snore . . . real loud!

Signed,
Get-Real Girl

THE FIRST FORM BUZZ
by Dana Woletsky

I just learned something in American History that made my head spin. Did you know that in the 1600s they used to dunk the village *gossip*?

What were they thinking? Gossip is an important part of American history. Didn't Paul Revere do it when he told us the British were coming? And why did Alexander Graham Bell invent the telephone? To order a pizza? I don't think so!

But don't expect *this* gossip to call it quits. Because have I got news for you!

For starters, a new contest rules at Porter House. Love-struck First Formers are making lists of Harrington boys they like, and – you guessed it – the longest list wins. Word has it that AB doesn't just have a list – she has a computer printout! Wowee!

And speaking of winners, *Bye Bye Birdie* was a major hit! But another little birdie told me that a certain understudy (initials VM) was spotted backstage wearing MKB's costume! Was she just posing? Or did VM have more up her sleeve than just her arm?

Oh, well. Gotta fly. This hottie from Harrington just walked into the newsroom. And his initials are – C.U.T.E.!

The Buzz Girl

UPCOMING CALENDAR

Be afraid! Be very afraid! No, it's not the White Oak Ghost – it's those final

exams heading our way the first three weeks in December. So stock up on chocolate-chip cookies and cram, baby, cram!

News flash! There is life after final exams! The end-of-term pizza party will be held on December 21st at 7:00 p.m. in the common room. Get ready to pump up the music – and the pepperoni!

What better way to chill with Harrington boys than

at the annual Winter Festival on January 10th? There'll be games, contests and if the cocoa isn't hot enough – plenty of adorable guys!

Spring is in the air! So whether you crave romance – or just love to dance – head to the Spring

Fling Dance on April 18th. There'll be plenty of flower power and all your best mates!

Summer may be hazy and crazy – but never lazy! Sign up now for the White Oak Summer Getaway! Rumour has it that this year campers will be headed for Florida. So bring your swimsuit and watch out for those alligators!

Winter Horoscopes

Capricorn:
(December 2–January 19)

Hey, groovy goat-girl! You don't always have to follow the herd. Be your own person and do the things *you* want to do! Got an urge to eat your pizza backwards? Go for it! Want to wear your bunny slippers to the next dance? Hop to it! Tired of wearing your hair like your best friend's? Try a brand new do! Just remember to be the best person you can be. Be YOU!

Aquarius:
(January 20–February 18)

Water Bearers carry more than just H_2O on their shoulders – they carry the world! So if your schedule is exploding with soccer, drama club, pizza parties, the shopping, and more – TIME OUT!! Take a quiet walk on campus and listen to your thoughts. Write long letters to your mates at home. Give yourself a hot-pink pedicure! But most of all, stop and smell the roses. Or if it's still winter – the hot chocolate!

Pisces:
(February 19–March 20)

Lucky Pisces – you're always stuffed to the gills with big dreams! And everyone knows the best part of dreams is making them come true! So whether you want to be a surgeon, a whale trainer, a fashion designer, or a straight-A student, don't let anyone stand between you and your goals. And keep on dreaming. Just snap out of it in the maths lesson!

PSST! Take a sneak peek
at

It's Snow Problem

Ashley reached Mary-Kate's door and knocked.

"Enter!" her sister's voice called.

Ashley went inside. She didn't see Mary-Kate anywhere. "Mary-Kate? Where are you?"

"Down here!"

Ashley looked down and saw Mary-Kate lying on the floor, her arms out in a "T" position. She held her history textbook in one hand and her English textbook in the other and was lifting them in the air in a circle. Up, down, up, down . . .

"What are you doing?" Ashley demanded.

"Lifting weights," Mary-Kate explained breathlessly. "Six sets of twelve. Then I'm going to do bicep curls and tricep kick-backs and ab crunches."

Ashley plopped down on Mary-Kate's bed. "Why are you doing this?"

"Just because I can't practise with my Winter

Festival teams doesn't mean I can't stay in shape," Mary-Kate said. She put the books down with a loud thump. "I have to be ready to compete in case you find the goat thief by Friday. Have you found the goat thief?" she added hopefully.

Ashley hesitated before answering. She wished that she had some good news for Mary-Kate, but she didn't.

The Harrington School for Boys and White Oak Academy were competing in the Winter Festival. And both sides were playing tricks on the other. Mary-Kate had been thrown out of the festival because someone found the Harrington mascot – a goat – in her room!

Ashley knew Mary-Kate hadn't stolen the goat. She had been set up. But who was the real culprit?

"I haven't found out anything," Ashley admitted. "But I'm working on it."

Mary-Kate looked upset. Ashley was about to lean over and give her a hug when she noticed something.

On the floor near where Mary-Kate was doing her exercises was a crumpled piece of paper.

Ashley leaned over to pick it up. "What's this?" she asked Mary-Kate.

Mary-Kate glanced at it and shrugged. "Oh, it's probably one of Campbell's failed three-point shots."

"Oh," Ashley unfolded the paper. It was a piece of stationery bordered by black stars, asteroids and space ships. In the middle of the page, in purple Magic Marker, was written: PORTER 12.

What does that mean? Ashley wondered. *Is it some kind of code?*

She showed the piece of paper to Mary-Kate. "Did you write this?"

Mary-Kate stared at the piece of paper and frowned. "Uh, no, I don't think so. I don't recognize that stationery, either."

"Porter twelve, Porter twelve," Ashley muttered. And then it came to her like a lightning bolt. "Porter twelve! That's your room number."

"Oh, yeah," Mary-Kate said, nodding.

"This was written by someone who wanted to find your room," Ashley explained. "As in someone who wanted to find your room and leave a goat in it!"

"We've found the goat thief!" Mary-Kate practically screamed.

Already Ashley's mental wheels were spinning. She had a plan. And if her plan worked, Mary-Kate's name would be cleared by this time tomorrow.

Just in time for the festival!

mary-kateandashley

Coming soon – can you collect them all?

(1)	It's a Twin Thing	(0 00 714480 6)
(2)	How to Flunk Your First Date	(0 00 714479 2)
(3)	The Sleepover Secret	(0 00 714478 4)
(4)	One Twin Too Many	(0 00 714477 6)
(5)	To Snoop or Not to Snoop	(0 00 714476 8)
(6)	My Sister the Supermodel	(0 00 714475 X)
(7)	Two's a Crowd	(0 00 714474 1)
(8)	Let's Party	(0 00 714473 3)
(9)	Calling All Boys	(0 00 714472 5)
(10)	Winner Take All	(0 00 714471 7)
(11)	PS Wish You Were Here	(0 00 714470 9)
(12)	The Cool Club	(0 00 714469 5)
(13)	War of the Wardrobes	(0 00 714468 7)
(14)	Bye-Bye Boyfriend	(0 00 714467 9)
(15)	It's Snow Problem	(0 00 714466 0)
(16)	Likes Me, Likes Me Not	(0 00 714465 2)
(17)	Shore Thing	(0 00 714464 4)
(18)	Two for the Road	(0 00 714463 6)

 HarperCollins*Entertainment*

 PARACHUTE PRESS

 DUALSTAR PUBLICATIONS

 mary-kateandashley.com
AOL Keyword: mary-kateandashley

TM & © 2002 Dualstar Entertainment Group, LLC.

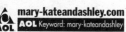

Mary-Kate and Ashley in their latest movie adventure

Available on video from 11th March

mary-kateandashley.com
AOL keyword: mary-kateandashley

DUALSTAR VIDEO

Get ready to celebrate with the

Real Dolls for Real Girls

Mary-Kate & Ashley Birthday Bash Fashion Dolls!

Celebrate with birth-day cake, present, and a camera to capture the memories!

Plus a hip floral halter dress included for trendy birthday style!

DUALSTAR CONSUMER PRODUCTS

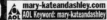 mary-kateandashley

mary-kateandashley.com
AOL Keyword: mary-kateandashley

 MATTEL

Mary-Kate and Ashley's latest exciting movie adventure

Available to own on video and DVD 29th July 2002

DUALSTAR VIDEO

AOL mary-kateandashley.com
AOL Keyword: mary-kateandashley

It's What YOU Watch!

AOL mary-kateandashley.com
AOL Keyword: mary-kateandashley

CLUB Acclaim

Real Books for Real Girls.

It's What **YOU** Read

b the 1st 2 kno
mary-kateandashley

REGISTER 4 THE HARPERCOLLINS AND MK&ASH TEXT CLUB AND KEEP UP2 D8 WITH THE L8EST MK&ASH BOOK NEWS AND MORE.

SIMPLY TEXT TOK, FOLLOWED BY YOUR GENDER (M/F), DATE OF BIRTH (DD/MM/YY) AND POSTCODE TO: 07786277301.

SO, IF YOU ARE A GIRL BORN ON THE 12TH MARCH 1986 AND LIVE IN THE POSTCODE DISTRICT RG19 YOUR MESSAGE WOULD LOOK LIKE THIS: TOKF120386RG19.

IF YOU ARE UNDER 14 YEARS WE WILL NEED YOUR PARENTS' OR GUARDIANS' PERMISSION FOR US TO CONTACT YOU. PLEASE ADD THE LETTER 'G' TO THE END OF YOUR MESSAGE TO SHOW YOU HAVE YOUR PARENTS' CONSENT. LIKE THIS: TOKF120386RG19G.

HarperCollins*Entertainment*

PARACHUTE PRESS

DUALSTAR PUBLICATIONS

mary-kateandashley.com
AOL Keyword: mary-kateandashley

TM & © 2002 Dualstar Entertainment Group, Inc.

Order Form

To order direct from the publishers, just make a list of the titles you want and fill in the form below:

Name ....

Address ....

....

....

Send to: Dept 6, HarperCollins Publishers Ltd, Westerhill Road, Bishopbriggs, Glasgow G64 2QT.

Please enclose a cheque or postal order to the value of the cover price, plus:

UK & BFPO: Add £1.00 for the first book, and 25p per copy for each additional book ordered.

Overseas and Eire: Add £2.95 service charge. Books will be sent by surface mail but quotes for airmail despatch will be given on request.

A 24-hour telephone ordering service is available to holders of Visa, MasterCard, Amex or Switch cards on 0141- 772 2281.

An imprint of **HarperCollins***Publishers*